Welcome to the world of Beast Quest!

Tom was once an ordinary village boy, until he travelled to the City, met King Hugo and discovered his destiny. Now he is the Master of the Beasts, sworn to defend Avantia and its people against Evil. Tom draws on the might of the magical Golden Armour, and is protected by powerful tokens granted to him by the Good Beasts of Avantia. Tom and his loyal companion Elenna are always ready to visit new lands and tackle the enemies of the realm.

While there's blood in his veins, Tom will never give up the Quest…

BLOOD VALLEY

FROZEN LAKE

KROTAX
THE TUSKED
DESTROYER

BY ADAM BLADE

With special thanks to Allan Frewin Jones

For Theo Dare – never stop seeking adventure!

www.beastquest.co.uk

ORCHARD BOOKS

First published in Great Britain in 2019 by The Watts Publishing Group

1 3 5 7 9 10 8 6 4 2

Text © 2019 Beast Quest Limited.
Cover and inside illustrations by Steve Sims
© Beast Quest Limited 2019

Beast Quest is a registered trademark of Beast Quest Limited
Series created by Beast Quest Limited, London

A CIP catalogue record for this book is available from the British Library.

ISBN 978 1 40834 345 6

Printed in Great Britain

The paper and board used in this book are made from wood from responsible sources

Orchard Books
An imprint of Hachette Children's Group
Part of The Watts Publishing Group Limited
Carmelite House, 50 Victoria Embankment, London EC4Y 0DZ

An Hachette UK Company
www.hachette.co.uk
www.hachettechildrens.co.uk

There are special gold coins to collect in this book. You will earn one coin for every chapter you read.

Find out what to do with your coins at the end of the book.

CONTENTS

It's been many years since I crossed the borders of Avantia. I can't say I've missed the place much. Last time I was here, my plan to conquer the kingdom was foiled by a mere boy, though he calls himself their Master of the Beasts.

Now I serve a new and cruel master. Though he looks like a man, he has the cold heart of a monster. We have travelled day and night from the Wildlands north of Avantia's frozen wastes, and at last the walls of the City loom into view.

I have heard the boy Tom is still alive. I wonder what he will think when he sees me again. And I wonder if he will understand the terrible danger that is about to be unleashed.

One thing is certain – the kingdom and its people are going to suffer a terrible fate.

Yours,

Kapra the Witch

THE SACRIFICE

"Little hero!" roared Carwin, the tribal chief. "See how he endures the sting of my daughter's ointment!"

"It doesn't sting at all," said Tom, smiling at the girl kneeling at his side. She scooped more of the thick paste out of her stone pounding bowl and smoothed it on to his wounded arm. "Thank you, Lika."

He and Elenna sat with the northern free folk around a blazing fire, wrapped in fur blankets while their clothes dried on a wicker frame. An old warrior stirred delicious-smelling stew in a large pot hung over the flames.

Elenna leaned towards Tom. "These are the most civilised barbarians I've ever met," she murmured.

Tom nodded. When they had travelled through Daltec's portal to the northern Wildlands, they had been expecting to confront a hostile tribe. Tom looked around the circle of tall, muscular men and women. Apart from their leather and fur clothes, and their wild

braided hair, there was nothing very
fearsome about these people. They
had welcomed Tom and Elenna
after they had defeated Querzol,
a monstrous Beast who terrorised
the nearby swamps. The battle had

been a desperate trial for Tom — for the first time in many Quests, he had to fight without his jewelled belt, his shield tokens or the power of his Golden Armour.

"Querzol was just one of the four Beasts that haunt our land," Carwin said grimly. "You will need our help if you are to destroy the other three." He leaned forward. "But tell us why you came here."

"It's a horrible story," said Elenna. "Avantia's king, Hugo, has been on the throne since before we were born – but, all that time, he had an older brother."

"Angelo," said Tom, taking up the tale. "Everyone believed he had been killed in the war in the Wildlands."

Carwin frowned. "That war ended more than thirty years ago, when Angelo killed the chieftain, Uthrain. But Angelo disappeared after the battle – no one knows where."

"He recently returned to Avantia, accompanied by a witch named Kapra." Tom glanced at Carwin, but the barbarian seemed not to recognise the name. "King Hugo offered his brother the crown, and Angelo took it. But we learned very quickly that the new king had become cruel and greedy."

"Maybe Kapra put a spell on him?" Elenna suggested.

"Possibly," said Tom. "Or perhaps

something corrupted him in the lost years."

"Angelo said that the realm no longer needed a Master of the Beasts now they had a mighty new king," said Elenna, shuddering at the memory. "Tom was declared an enemy of the kingdom, and was imprisoned."

"Kapra took the magic tokens from my shield," Tom added, showing them the slight indentations on the bare wood of his shield. "She confiscated my jewelled belt, and my Golden Armour was melted before my eyes. I was about to be executed when Elenna came to my rescue."

"The Good Wizard Daltec conjured a portal that brought us here," continued Elenna. "We are searching for the truth about Angelo."

While they spoke, the stew was ladled into wooden bowls. Tom ate with relish – it was a delicious mixture of rabbit, mushrooms and herbs.

"Most of the people who fought in the war are dead," said Carwin. "But the son of Uthrain still lives." He pointed towards the distant hills. "His name is Jax and he is the leader of the Blood Valley Tribe."

"Will you guide us to him?" Tom asked.

Carwin's brow furrowed and he and the other barbarians stared uneasily into the fire.

"The Blood Valley Tribe are the terror of all other tribes in the Wildlands," said Lika. She paused, looking at her father as though she was not sure she should speak of such things. "They demand a cruel sacrifice from every tribe—"

Her words were interrupted by the sudden thud of hoofbeats. A few of the men leaped up, staring towards the approaching horses as they emerged from the darkness.

A red banner flapped in the firelight. A harsh voice rang out. "I would speak with Carwin of the Mangrove Tribe!"

"I am here!" cried Carwin. He quickly turned to Tom and Elenna.

"Conceal yourselves," he hissed, gesturing towards the hide-covered huts that ringed the fire.

Tom and Elenna crept into one, crouching at the entrance and peering through the leather flaps to see a small group of horsemen approaching. Their hair was ragged, their faces stern, and their belts loaded with weapons that glinted in the firelight.

Carwin stood up and walked towards the horsemen. "Why do you come here, Sharg of the Blood Valley Tribe?"

Sharg threw a sack at Carwin's feet. "Your tribute is past due," he growled. "And Krotax is hungry."

Carwin's shoulders slumped. "Do
not threaten us with the Beast. You
shall have your sacrifice."

Tom and Elenna glanced
uncertainly at one another,
wondering what all this meant.

Carwin lifted the sack. The
tribesfolk walked silently past him
and reached into the sack, each
drawing out a shard of white bone.
One by one, each barbarian sighed
with relief, then dropped their bone

on the ground.

Now it was Lika's turn. The bone she drew out was black. Her face drained of colour. A groan sounded

from the others.

"No!" Carwin stepped forward, pushing Lika behind him. "Take me instead!"

"The Sacred Bones choose the sacrifice, not you, Carwin of the Mangrove Tribe," shouted Sharg.

Tom noticed a few of the tribesfolk fingering their weapons and eyeing the horsemen with grim defiance.

"Step aside, or face the wrath of Krotax!" Sharg demanded.

Hands dropped from weapons and sorrow and fear twisted their faces as some of the elders drew Carwin aside.

"All will be well," Lika murmured, kissing her father. "Protect our people." She walked towards Sharg, her face pale but her head held high.

Sharg dragged her up into the saddle behind him. The horsemen turned and rode away.

Tom and Elenna ran to where Carwin stood, his head in his hands, surrounded by his grieving people.

"Why did you let them take her?" demanded Tom.

"She is to be gifted to the Beast," Carwin groaned. "The Blood Valley Tribe takes sacrifices from all the other tribes of the Wildlands. If we refuse, they will set the Beast free, and all will die!"

1

RESCUE

Tom looked bravely at Carwin. "I'll bring Lika back to you," he said. "And I will end the Blood Valley Tribe's reign of terror!"

The chieftain's face was full of doubt.

"I defeated Querzol," Tom reminded him.

"Krotax is a sterner test," replied

Carwin. "It is said that before he was snared by the Blood Valley Tribe, he laid waste to entire villages."

Tom stared at Carwin in alarm. "Then I will fight all the harder!" he declared.

"And I will be by his side," added Elenna. "Just tell us where we can find this monster."

A flicker of hope lit Carwin's face. "Perhaps you do have the heart to defeat the four Beasts of the Wildlands, though you are only small," he said. He pointed towards distant hills, black under the night sky. "There is a path through the high lands that is too steep and narrow for a horse to pass."

Tom paused for a moment, asking himself if he really thought he could defeat such a foe without his magic powers.

"Then that is where we will go," he said, shaking off his doubts. "There isn't a moment to lose!"

"This is perfect for an ambush," hissed Tom. They had followed Carwin's instructions and had come to a lofty tooth of rock where the mountain road narrowed.

The small band of Blood Valley men on their horses was moving along the narrow road below in single file. Lika drooped in the

saddle behind the burly figure of
Sharg.

Tom picked up a rock in either
hand. "I'll aim for the leader," he told
Elenna. "You take down as many as
you can."

Elenna nodded, picking up two
more rocks.

The horsemen passed under them.
Tom flung the rock with all his
strength. It struck Sharg on the side
of the head, sending him tumbling
out of his saddle.

One of Elenna's rocks hit a second
rider in the chest and he rolled
backwards off his horse with a cry.

The horses reared and neighed
in panic. Two of them bolted back

down the path, their riders clinging
on helplessly. But another barbarian
mastered his horse and drew his
sword, staring up.

Elenna didn't hesitate. With a yell, she launched herself off the crag and plunged down at the horseman. Her feet caught him full in the chest, smashing him off his horse as she tucked and rolled to safety.

Tom leaped at the final rider. But the barbarian jerked the reins and the horse backed away. Tom crashed painfully to the ground, twisting his ankle as he landed.

He lay gasping for breath, his ankle throbbing. *I must be careful from now on*, he reminded himself. *I no longer have my green jewel to mend broken bones*.

With a snarl, the horseman slid from the saddle and swung his sword.

Tom rolled clear. Ignoring the pain in his ankle, he sprang to his feet, raising his shield to deflect another swing of the barbarian's blade. He drew his own sword, slashing at his enemy, but the barbarian danced aside, grinning as he swung again. The blow struck Tom's shield, forcing him backwards, always on the defensive.

His heel struck rock. *Nowhere to go...*

He dropped to his knees, covering his head with his shield. The barbarian gave a bark of laughter as he brought his sword down. Tom dived aside and lashed out with both feet, sweeping the barbarian's legs from under him.

The swordsman fell, striking his head on stone.

Tom stood over his fallen foe, panting, but triumphant. He saw Elenna tying up another of the barbarians. One already lay with his arms bound behind his back.

"You fools!" cried Lika.

Tom stared in astonishment as she leaped down from the horse. "We just rescued you!" he said.

"And condemned my whole tribe to death!" replied Lika. "If the sacrifice is not made, Jax will set Krotax free and no one will be safe!"

Tom frowned at her. "While there is blood in my veins, I won't let that happen."

There was a growl of mocking laughter. One of the bound captives staggered to his feet.

"Blood in your veins, little boy?" he laughed. "Krotax will drink your

blood before he crunches your puny
bones!"

Tom ignored the taunts. He'd heard
too many enemies predict his death
to care what one more defeated
barbarian thought.

"How far is it to his tribe's village?"
he asked Lika.

"It isn't a village, it's a fortress,"
Lika replied. "It's a short morning's
ride away. I will guide you."

They gathered the three remaining
horses and rode on, leaving the bound
men behind. They'd get free in time,
but not soon enough to hamper the
Quest.

The pass opened out and wound
down into a scrubby plain, bordered

by distant grey mountains. A bleak, whining wind ripped at the tall grasses and bit through Tom's clothes as he and Elenna rode either side of the silent Lika.

"In Avantia, Angelo told us there were four Beasts in the Wildlands – but that he personally had defeated one," Elenna said, looking at Lika.

Lika frowned. "I think he was lying. You dealt with Querzol, but there are still three left: Krotax, Torka and Xerkan." She shuddered.

"That's another part of Angelo's story that makes no sense," Tom said. "We can't trust anything he told us!"

"What's Krotax like?" asked Elenna.

Lika blushed. "I've never actually

seen him, and those who have tend
to reach the end of their lives soon
after. He is said to have skin and
teeth of metal. To feel no pain, only
rage. He has no mercy."

Tom felt his heart beat faster.

Krotax sounded utterly terrifying. Not for the first time, he doubted the wisdom of his Quest. Without his powers, he was just a boy.

He gripped the reins tighter and pushed his fears aside.

This kingdom has no Master of the Beasts. Its people are defenceless. I cannot turn away...

TAMING THE BEAST

When they reached the top of a
low hill, Tom caught his first sight
of the Blood Valley Tribe's fortress.
His spirits sank further. It was an
enormous palisade of tree trunks
reaching out from mountainous
cliffs, and within the curve of the
wooden wall, he saw the rooftops of
many buildings. Smoke trailed into

the sky. The whipping wind carried harsh shouting and the sound of hammers on anvils and swords on whetstones.

"They are always preparing for war," Lika murmured. "Are you sure you want to do this?"

Tom stared at the bustling fortress, wondering if he could succeed without his magical powers.

He saw Elenna watching him anxiously.

He sat up straight, squaring his shoulders. "Yes," he said, his hand on his sword hilt. "I am sure."

"Well, we can't enter by the gates," said Lika. "We'll be outnumbered straight away and fed to Krotax!"

Tom noticed a stretch of tall grasses that led almost to the walls.

"We'll leave the horses and go that way," he said, pointing.

They dismounted, keeping low until they reached cover.

They moved cautiously through the waving grasses, careful not to reveal themselves. They were almost upon the fortress now.

The wooden wall towered over them, the tip of each tree trunk sharpened to a point. Two ox-drawn carts trundled along a road that led to the fortified gates. The carts were open, and bound prisoners huddled in the back.

"More sacrifices for the Beast,"

Lika hissed in Tom's ear. "On this day each year, all the tribes must give up one of their loved ones."

"We have to rescue them," said Elenna.

"Not yet," said Tom. "We need to get into the fortress first. Then we can make our plans."

Lika looked doubtfully at him. "Getting in may not be difficult," she murmured. "Getting out again is impossible."

"Nothing is impossible," Tom replied. "Follow me – we'll use the carts as cover."

They dashed through the grasses. The carts had high wheels and the oxen moved slowly. Tom dived under

the leading cart.

He glanced back. He could just see Elenna and Lika under the second cart.

So far, so good.

Tom gripped his sword hilt as the carts approached the open gates. There were guards everywhere, dressed in reeking animal skins, tattoos darkening their hairy arms and faces, swords and axes in their hands.

They passed through the gates without being seen and came into a bustling forecourt hemmed by huts and workshops. People milled about the carts, calling out to the captives, mocking them.

This is a fortress of horrors, thought Tom.

"Where's that lazy brute Sharg with the Mangrove sacrifice?" someone called.

"Never mind!" replied a harsh voice. "The shaman says we cannot wait any longer."

Tom slipped from under the cart and ducked into a narrow alley between a blacksmith's forge and an open-sided warehouse filled with piles of stinking animal hides. Moments later, Elenna and Lika were beside him. Lika's face was pale, but there was courage in her eyes.

"We need to blend in," Tom said, taking three hides from the piles. "Hold your nose if you must." He pulled a reeking skin over his shoulders.

Tom peered around the corner

of the smithy and saw the carts trundling along a road that led towards the rearing mountainside.

Many of the barbarian folk followed the carts, clapping one another on the back and letting out raucous cheers.

Tom and his companions joined the throng as the carts edged between huts and rough-hewn wooden buildings. They came to a heavy, slatted fence that surrounded a wide area of beaten earth at the foot of the massive cliff. A huge rock stood against the mountainside, anchored in place by a system of chains and pulleys embedded high in the rockface. A gate was opened and the carts trundled in. Armed men dragged the captives down. The assembled crowd spread out behind the fence, peering through the slats. Tom eyed the huge rock uneasily. He had a feeling he knew what was on the other side.

The crowd quietened as two figures stepped into the open. In the lead was a shrivelled old man dressed in grubby hides, wearing a feathered headdress and a heavy necklace of bleached bones. *He must be the shaman they were speaking of.* As the man shuffled slowly towards the rock, he swung a metal urn on a chain, belching thick white smoke. Following him was a giant of a man with thick, knotted muscles and a bald head covered in black tattoos.

The crowd was silent now, watchful and waiting as the old man drew to a stop before the rock, still swinging the urn.

Lika leaned close to Tom's ear. "The big one is Jax," she whispered.

Even as she spoke, Jax drew his sword and gestured to the men holding the captives. The weeping victims were pushed forward.

Tom fought the urge to race to their aid, reminding himself that he was without his magical powers, in enemy territory, surrounded by armed men – with some kind of Beast lurking behind that boulder.

It would be brains, not brawn, that won the day.

Jax raised his arms. "Open it!" he bellowed.

Six barbarians ran forward, snatching up the chains and heaving.

Slowly, the boulder rose into the air with the screech of stone on stone. Some of the captives fell wailing to their knees as a massive dark hole opened up in the rock.

Tom peered into the darkness, holding his breath as he waited to get a glimpse of the terrible menace for the first time.

Jax raised both arms, his voice bellowing out. "Great Krotax, the sacred time is nigh! Prepare to feast upon the lives I have brought for you!"

Tom's heart pounded in the dreadful silence that followed Jax's call. All eyes were locked on the gaping cave mouth.

Deep snorting and bellowing echoed from the chasm.

A dim shape moved in the darkness.

The old man walked hesitantly towards the cave mouth, still swinging the incense urn as the gloom swallowed him.

"Surely he'll be killed!" whispered Elenna.

Jax followed the shaman.

The bellowing grew louder, then stopped abruptly.

Could the old man be a Beast Keeper, like Wilfred from Rion? Tom wondered, as he saw a snake rear up in the cave mouth. No! Not a snake – it was the huge trunk of a great armoured hill of flesh and matted fur.

A monstrous woolly mammoth stomped out into the daylight. The crowd gasped in awe. The prisoners cried out and flung themselves to the ground.

Tom shrank back from the dreadful sight. Krotax was immense, his great curved tusks sharpened to scimitar edges, his trunk bound by spiked bands of iron. Huge metal plates hung from his sides and an iron helmet covered his colossal head, hiding his eyes. The urn swung from his neck, the white smoke rising up around his face.

Perched high on the massive shoulders, Jax the barbarian chieftain

pulled at the blind Beast's leather
reins.

"Bring forth our offerings!" Jax
called. "Let Krotax eat his fill!"

4

BREAKING THE SPELL

The mammoth stamped his hooves, shaking the ground. The armour rattled and clanged on his flanks. He raised his trunk and bellowed, spittle spraying from his gaping mouth.

If ever I needed all my powers, it's now! Tom thought as he gaped at the monster. Jax looked tiny perched on the Beast's great neck.

Lika leaned towards Tom. "The burning incense tames Krotax so he can be ridden," she murmured.

The captives were prodded forward at spear-point. A man fell and was dragged to his feet again. A young woman cried out for help, but the gathered crowd just laughed back at her.

"Let's see what happens without the incense," said Elenna, fitting arrow to bow. She took aim and fired, the arrow striking the urn, sending it tumbling away in a cloud of white smoke.

A stunned silence came down over the fortress as the rolling urn came to a stop. As the smoke drifted away, the mammoth grunted and snorted, shaking his head.

Jax struggled with the reins, his face twisted with fear and anger. "How do I control the Beast?" he shouted down at the old man in the headdress.

But the shaman had already turned and ran as fast as his weak legs would carry him, as Krotax gave a roar that shook the mountainside.

"He's waking up!" Tom gasped.

A moment later, the Beast thrashed his massive trunk from side to side, his mouth a vast red chasm as he let out bellow after bellow. He reared up on his hind legs, throwing Jax to

the ground as cries and howls rose from the crowd. The tribe leader rolled aside, only just avoiding the pounding hooves as they came crashing down.

The Beast trumpeted in fury, swinging his trunk like a giant club, chasing away the men who had been guarding the captives.

Jax got to his feet, raising his arms. "Krotax! Heed me! I am Jax of the Blood Valley Tribe!" The Beast snorted, his head turning as he blindly stretched his trunk towards the voice.

Jax sprang aside and darted for the incense burner, but Krotax lashed out with his trunk, striking the huge barbarian across the shoulders and sending him spinning.

Tom watched in awe as the chieftain, dwarfed by the mountainous Beast, ran for the fence, vaulting over it only a moment before the Beast blindly crashed through. Tom ducked as shards of wood flew through the air.

"How do we fight him?" shouted Elenna.

"We don't, for now," Tom called back. "We have to free the captives!"

Taking his lead, Elenna and Lika shoved their way through the stampeding crowds.

They clambered over the fence, their movements hampered by the animal hides, and ran for the huddled prisoners. Tom drew his sword, cutting through their bonds. "Go!" he urged them. "Get away from here!"

"Thank you," called a young woman as she ran, though others were speechless with fear.

Tom turned to the Beast. Krotax was rampaging beyond the broken fence, his tusks ripping through huts, his hooves smashing everything in his path.

A few soldiers stood their ground, hurling javelins at the mammoth. Some sank into his thick hair, but most rattled off the armour. Krotax turned, swinging his spiked trunk, sending up fountains of splintered wood. A hoof came down on a cart, obliterating it.

One of the soldiers dipped an arrow into a fire and sent it flying towards the Beast's face. It glanced off the helmet and sank into Krotax's shoulder.

Trumpeting in rage and pain, Krotax turned and pounded away, desperate to escape the flames. But in his blind rage, he ran headlong into the mountainside.

There was a deafening *clang* as the great helmet struck the rock. Krotax staggered back, the hair around his neck smoking. The impact had snuffed out the flames and Tom saw that the helmet had been split in two. Krotax shook his head and the pieces fell away. Now, at last, the Beast could see.

The massive head turned towards Tom, and he saw a deep malice in the mammoth's red eyes.

"Tom, behind you!" Lika's voice rang out at his back. He turned just in time to deflect a blow from a sword. A few warriors were trying to stop the captives from escaping. Elenna fired arrows, keeping them at bay while the prisoners clung together.

As Tom fought, he saw Lika crouch and spin, her outstretched leg sweeping two warriors off their feet. An axe missed her by a hair's breadth as she somersaulted backwards, kicking out and felling the attacker like a rotten tree trunk.

She spun towards Tom and made a sudden spring, her hands on his shoulders as she boosted herself over his head. There was a grunt and Tom turned in time to see an axe-wielding barbarian go down with both of Lika's feet in his face.

"You're welcome!" she panted, jumping up.

Another barbarian held a captive woman by the throat. With an angry cry, Lika launched herself at the man and defeated him.

Tom parried the thrust of a spear and swung around in time to block

a jabbing sword with his shield. But
a hard blow on his back sent him
tumbling across the ground.

Clawing dirt out of his eyes,
Tom got to his knees. A burly
figure struck at him from the side.
A weapon came swinging down.
Instinctively, Tom warded it off with
his shield, but the blow almost drove
him on to his face.

He rolled away and leaped up,
sword and shield raised.

He found himself staring up at Jax.
The barbarian swung two axes as he
glared down at Tom.

"I do not know who you and
your companions are," howled the
furious chieftain. "But I know you

are responsible for this outrage! Die
now, pathetic boy!"

"I may be a boy," Tom shouted

defiantly, "but I have brought down bigger foes than you in my time!"

But not without any of my powers, he thought, warily watching as the barbarian surged forward, his axes spinning with deadly force.

5

DEATH TRAP

Tom leaped back as the two blades dug into the ground. He might not have had the power of his golden armour, but he had fighting skills honed in countless battles.

While Jax fought to pull the axe-heads free, Tom launched himself forward, jumping over the axes to slam his shield into Jax's face.

Jax staggered back, roaring in
agony and bleeding from his nose,
before ducking forward, wrenching

the axe-heads free and swinging them both at Tom.

With two swift swipes of his sword, Tom knocked the axes aside in a shower of sparks. He jabbed with his blade, but Jax bounded back and spun on his heel, the two axes whipping through the air.

Tom leaped over one axe, but the blade of the other smashed into his shield, making him stumble back and almost lose his footing.

Jax stalked towards him, his face ablaze with battle-fury.

Tom retreated, his shield blocking blow after blow, pain flaring through his arms. His strength was waning and his heart pounded. His legs felt heavy and clumsy. When his back foot trod on something that moved under his weight, the world around him reeled as he stumbled, fighting for balance.

He looked down and saw he had stepped on the incense burner, still belching the strange-smelling smoke, which quickly made him feel dizzy. He stumbled, coughing and spluttering, his will to fight slipping away, but for a moment Jax was hidden from view.

Tom dropped to one knee. From the corner of his eye, he saw Krotax slamming his great armoured body into the fence as he tossed barbarians into the air with his spiked trunk. Lika and Elenna were guiding the terrified prisoners towards a large hut.

At the last second, Tom saw an axe cutting towards his neck. He just managed to block the blow with the rim of his shield, but the impact knocked him on to his face. He sprawled, gasping for breath, wracked with pain.

Jax grinned in triumph, stepping towards Tom. "Prepare to meet your doom!" howled the barbarian chief, raising both axes.

Desperately, Tom clawed up some dirt and flung it into Jax's face. The barbarian staggered back. Tom leaped to his feet, coughing and spitting to clear his lungs of the giddying smoke.

There was a shout, and Tom spun round to see a second barbarian running at him with a spear and a sword. Tom swept the spear-point aside, but the sword blade cut across his thigh. It was a shallow wound, but made him suck a breath at the sudden sharp pain.

In the past, Tom would have quickly dispatched his enemy – even one as large as this brute. But without his powers, could he trust that skill would overcome brawn? He wavered, backing off as the barbarian came at him with jabbing spear and slashing blade.

Is magic the only reason I won so many battles?

Gathering all his strength, Tom slashed his sword at the wooden shaft, cutting it in two, and throwing the barbarian off-balance.

Then he drove his shoulder into his foe's gut, winding him. Finally, he slammed the butt of his sword-hilt against the brute's head, knocking him out cold.

Tom stood over him, panting, but triumphant.

I'm more than my lost powers! I am the Master of the Beasts!

"Surrender now and die swiftly, or fight on and die slowly!" howled a voice. Tom turned. Jax had recovered and his eyes burned with revenge. He hurled himself at Tom, an axe sweeping down.

Tom barely had time to lift his shield.

Crunch!

The axe-head sank into the rim of his shield. Tom wrenched frantically at it, but the blade was stuck fast.

Jax widened his stance, leaning back and lifting Tom off his feet. Tom kicked out as he was raised into the air, his arm burning as his weight swung from the shield.

Roaring, Jax tossed him from side to side, like a dog shaking a rat. Tom slashed wildly with his sword, but his blows couldn't reach the chieftain. He lost his grip on his shield and tumbled through the air to land with a jarring crash, the breath beaten from his lungs.

He had no time to recover, or get to his shield. Jax was coming for him.

Tom scrambled up, deflecting a blade before bringing his sword down on the haft. The wood split and the axe-head crashed to the ground with a dull *clang*.

Now it was axe against sword. But Tom's breath was rasping in his throat, and his limbs were beyond weary.

He deflected one attack but left himself open to a punch from Jax's huge fist, which struck his jaw, knocking him sideways and jarring the sword out of his hand.

Spitting blood, Tom stared dazedly up at the towering barbarian chieftain.

"Avantians always were mewling weaklings," Jax taunted.

Desperately, Tom scraped at the ground, hoping to blind the barbarian a second time. But his fingers closed on something hard

and cold. It was the chain from the
incense holder.

Grasping it, Tom leaned back and
swung. The incense burner struck
Jax on the side of the head and he
staggered back, howling in pain.
The ground began to shake beneath
Tom's feet, and the chieftain turned,

a sudden dread in his eyes. "Krotax, I am your mas—"

His voice was drowned out by the bellowing of the Beast as he swiped his trunk, catching Jax and throwing him into the air like a child's doll.

Tom winced as the barbarian chieftain crashed to the ground, his limbs splayed, his head twisted at a horrible angle.

The formidable chief of the Blood Valley Tribe was dead.

1

RAMPAGE

Tom raised his sword as the
mountain of flesh and bone towered
over him. Cries of shock and grief
rang out from the crowd as they saw
their leader killed by the berserk
Beast. Those who were not already
running for their lives threw down
their weapons and fled.

Krotax turned from Tom and

lumbered after them, bellowing
with blood lust as he began to
run, his massive hooves smashing
everything in his path. Tom saw
with a shock of horror that the
Beast was charging towards the hut
where Elenna and Lika had taken
the terrified prisoners.

Tom raced after him.

*Unless Krotax is distracted,
everyone inside will be killed!*

He didn't have the red jewel that
allowed him to speak to Beasts,
but still he shouted, desperate to
gain Krotax's attention and lure
him away from his friends. "Krotax,
stop! Fight me!"

His voice was lost in the Beast's

ferocious bellowing.

He saw Elenna at the hut's door, an arrow nocked. She fired, but the arrowhead skipped off the Beast's armour. Running away from the hut, she fired again. The arrow struck Krotax a glancing blow on his massive bony forehead. There was a splash of blood and the Beast roared in pain. It was a shallow wound, but it had drawn his attention.

Tom realised that his friend was making herself a target in order to save the others. *Brave, but reckless!* He worked his legs, dashing in Krotax's wake, determined to stand at Elenna's side.

"I'm with you!" he shouted. He

snatched up a fallen spear and flung it with all his strength. The blade glanced off the Beast's armour. Despite his bulk, Krotax was moving at a deadly speed, closing in on Elenna, his trunk raised and his fearsome tusks pointing right at her.

Tom grabbed up another spear and hurled it, striking the Beast's ankle. The sudden pain enraged Krotax. He turned, his furious red eyes seeking Tom as he stamped his feet until the ground shook.

Yes! Come and get me, you brute!

Lowering his head, Krotax charged, his sharpened tusks skimming the earth, his trunk lifted, the spikes bristling.

Tom held his ground, his heart thundering, the blood ringing in his ears louder than Krotax's roaring.

He waited as the armoured monster came closer and closer, until he could smell the foul breath and see the razor-sharp points of the tusks...

Not yet...wait... Now!

He leaped aside, vaulting a tusk, tucking himself into a ball and rolling across the ground as the Beast thundered past in clouds of dust.

Tom saw the axe that had fallen from Jax's hand lying close by. He snatched it up and swung it as Krotax made for him once more. The steel edge came down on a tusk, hacking through the ivory, but Krotax's foreleg caught Tom a glancing blow and he was flung headlong.

He crashed to the ground and lay still, his head pounding and his whole body wracked with pain. Krotax eyed him, his huge armoured flanks swelling as he snorted.

Then the Beast turned away.

Krotax thinks I'm dead!

Lika was standing close to the hut where the prisoners had been hidden. Tom saw Krotax break into a run, his trunk swaying, his one remaining tusk pointed at Lika's heart...

Tom sprang up. "Run, Lika!" he shouted. From the far side of the Beast, Elenna was firing arrows to try and gain Krotax's attention.

But the Beast ignored them both.

Lika's face was pale with terror as she turned and ran. Tom's heart sank – there was no way she could outrun the huge monster...

But then Tom saw that Lika was racing to catch up with a panicking horse. She leaped high, vaulting over the horse's rump and landing on its back. She snatched up the reins and pulled, jerking the horse's head to one side, forcing it to turn and race across Krotax's path.

Tom watched in dread as Lika urged the horse on, yanking on the reins again to come level with Krotax's flank. She rose out of the

saddle, crouching with her feet on
the terrified horse's back for just
a moment before she jumped up,
twisting in mid-air and taking hold
of the Beast's dangling reins. She
swarmed up the armour plate.

Forgetting all weariness and pain, amazed at her courage, Tom pursued the Beast.

I can't let her fight alone!

Krotax was still hurtling towards the hut where the prisoners had been hidden.

Even with her incredible skill and courage, what could Lika do to stop him?

Tom saw her crawl towards the Beast's neck, reaching up to yank back on the leather thongs and drag Krotax away from the hut.

The Beast roared, digging his hooves in and forcing a sudden stop. Caught off balance, Lika lost her grip and was flung over his head. She slammed into the ground, dust rising around her as she lay completely still.

A POINT OF
WEAKNESS

"No!" Tom cried, as he ran towards
Lika. The brave barbarian girl had
saved the prisoners, but at what
cost?

He glanced back in time to see an
arrow speed past Krotax's eyes. The
Beast turned his massive head to
glare at Elenna.

"I just need one lucky hit!" Elenna cried as she stood her ground and fired again.

Tom understood Elenna's plan – to distract Krotax while he checked on Lika. But what if she was already dead?

He stopped beside the barbarian girl, dropping to his knees. "Lika!"

Her face was twisted in pain, but her eyes were open. "My arm's broken," she groaned.

Tom helped her up. She cradled her useless arm, staring angrily at Krotax as he began to pace towards Elenna.

"You've done your part," Tom told her. "I have to finish Krotax now."

He stood up, steeling himself for the fight ahead.

"Wait!" Lika's voice was urgent.

"What is it?" asked Tom.

"When I was on the Beast's back, I saw a clasp," she called. "It's what holds his armour in place. One sword blow should break it."

Tom nodded. "Thank you." Then he pelted after the Beast, wondering how to get on to the mountainous back. With the power of his golden boots, it would have been simple – but without them, the jump was impossible.

Elenna was still firing arrows and running at the same time, pursued by Krotax. She reached the clearing where, earlier, the sacrifices had been offered to the Beast, then stopped with her back to the mountain face. She stared at the onrushing Beast as though she was paralysed with terror.

Trumpeting wildly, Krotax bore down on her. Tom's heart almost stopped. *She'll be crushed to death!*

At the last moment, Elenna rolled out of the way. Krotax smashed headlong into the cliff, the entire mountain shaking from the impact. The mammoth staggered backwards, shaking his head, snorting and roaring in pain.

Elenna took her chance to flee. The massive rock was poised above the cave, swinging on its chains.

Tom changed course, racing towards her as a plan formed in his mind. "Elenna!" he shouted. "When I tell you, fire at the winch that holds the rock!"

Tom ate up the ground to the cave mouth. Krotax stood under the cliff, moving his head slowly as though dazed.

"Krotax!" Tom yelled. "I am Avantia's Master of the Beasts – yield to me!"

The Beast turned, pounding along the cliff face, eyes burning and spiked trunk rearing as he gathered speed.

Tom felt a moment of fear.

If Elenna fails, I'll die here in this dark cave mouth.

Krotax thundered on. Tom's legs shook, and the blood rang in his ears. His weapons felt terribly heavy. He ached all over and he could feel his last reserves of strength draining away. The Beast was almost upon him, his bulk filling all of Tom's vision...

"Now!" he shouted to Elenna.

Tom heard the *twang* of the bowstring. The arrow arched into the air above the great stone. He heard the rattle of the loosened chains.

Tom threw himself sideways as the rock plunged down, smashing on to

Krotax's head, driving the Beast to
the ground.

Panting, Tom got to his feet.
Krotax lay on his side, his trunk

stretched out, his eyes closed. The
Beast was breathing hard, his flanks
heaving under the armour. The
creature's squinty eyes were dull.

Elenna ran to Tom's side.

"Nice shot," he said with a grim
smile.

Faces appeared from cover,
barbarian eyes wide as they stared
in shock at their fallen Beast. Lika
strode to the door of the captives'
hut and opened it.

"You can come out," she called.

They emerged, gazing at the
defeated mammoth as though they
could hardly believe their eyes. A
few of the people wept for joy and
others let out cheers.

Using the reins, Tom clambered up on to the Beast's back. Once up, he saw the clasp Lika had told him about. He raised his sword and broke it open with a single blow, the armour plate sliding away and striking the ground with a deep *clang*.

Tom saw that the heavy armour had worn away the hair on Krotax's sides, revealing raw and bloody skin. He winced at the sight — the enslaved Beast must have been in constant pain!

"Tom! Watch out!" Elenna's alarmed voice broke into his thoughts.

The trunk was twitching. A

moment later, it lifted and thumped down as Elenna sprang back. The huge head rose from the ground, the deadly eyes open wide once more and fixed on Tom.

Krotax surged up, trumpeting in fury. Tom staggered and slipped as Krotax got to his feet.

The Beast was not finished! He jabbed at Tom with his remaining tusk, knocking him sideways. Dazed, Tom scrambled out of reach as a mighty forefoot stamped down.

The Beast was groggy, but even so, Tom was only just able to avoid the pounding hooves as Krotax lurched after him.

Tom curled up, holding his shield

over his head. A sideswipe of the trunk flung him helplessly across the ground. His sword slipped from his fingers. Krotax stamped after him, trunk raised, spikes gleaming.

Can't get away...this time, I'm done for...

Krotax gave a bellow of agony and turned away. Elenna was firing arrows into the Beast's flank. They sank deep, arrow after arrow striking his exposed skin as he roared in pain. Krotax seemed confused. One moment he reared towards Tom, the next he turned to face Elenna and her arrows. With a bellow he moved towards her.

Tom saw a wooden stake from

the broken fence lying close by. *The point is sharp. I could use it as a spear.* Without the strength of the golden breastplate, though, he had no hope of lifting it alone. *But with help?*

He spun around, seeing the former prisoners huddled together.

"Help me," he called to them. "It's time to defeat Krotax!"

One or two ran forward, helping Tom lift the long stake. More joined

in, until there were a dozen of them, holding the stake like a battering ram.

"Now!" Tom shouted. They ran towards the Beast.

Elenna had her back to the mountain. Krotax was almost upon her.

"Quicker!" Tom urged, running faster, lifting the point of the stake.

A moment before Krotax reached Elenna, Tom and the prisoners drove the stake's point deep into the Beast's body.

Krotax's bellow of agony shook the cliff-face. His mighty head drooped, his legs buckling at the knees. The massive trunk dropped, smashing to the ground. With a final wheeze, the Beast sank to the earth, the red fire in his eyes dimming.

The scourge of the tribes was dead.

THE UNTOLD HISTORY

Tom was too weary to enjoy his victory. The death of any Beast never pleased him...but it was his duty to fight Evil wherever he found it, and to keep innocent people safe from harm.

The captives silently circled Krotax, afraid to get too close to a dead Beast. There was no sign of the barbarians of Blood Valley. All had fled.

Lika strode up, cradling her broken arm, but smiling broadly. "My father called you 'little hero'," she said. "But if courage and skill make heroes, then you are the greatest I have ever seen!"

"I would have failed without you and Elenna," Tom replied. "And your injury needs to be tended."

Lika laughed. "I've been hurt worse playing tag!"

Elenna's voice rang out. "It's the shaman!"

The bedraggled old man had crawled out from under an

upturned cart. His headdress hung in ruins around his face and there was blood on his cheek.

Wailing, he tottered to the dead Beast. "Mighty Krotax," he cried, "rise and smite these unbelievers!"

Some of the captives moved threateningly towards him.

Tom leaped in front of them. "No!" he commanded. "There's been enough death today."

They glared at Tom and he could see rage and disbelief in their expressions. "He would have fed us to the monster!" cried one man.

"And aren't you better than him?" asked Tom. "Go back to your people. Tell them that they will never again have to send sacrifices to the Blood Valley Tribe!"

The captives muttered among themselves, and some spat towards the cowering shaman, but then they turned and walked away.

Tom approached the shaman. "Get to your feet."

The old man grovelled on the ground. "Spare me," he wept. "I was obeying the orders of my chieftain." He stared at the Beast's body. "My beloved Krotax is dead – do not kill me, too."

Lika's lip curled, but Elenna stepped forward and helped the shaman to his feet.

"We won't kill you," she said.

Hope ignited in the old man's face. "You will answer my questions," Tom said firmly, fixing his gaze on the old man's watery eyes.

"Yes, yes – anything," he muttered.

"Tell me about the final battle in the war between your people and Avantia's Prince Angelo," Tom demanded.

The old man shook his head. "I cannot speak of that."

Lika's eyes glinted. "I am not from the civilised south, old man," she snarled. "If you don't answer this boy's questions, I will not hesitate to kill you where you stand."

The shaman eyed her in alarm. "My tale is not for all ears." He pointed at Tom. "I will speak to you alone."

"Very well," agreed Tom.

"Come," said the shaman. "I will show you the truth."

"I'll splint Lika's arm while you're gone," Elenna said.

The old man led Tom through a small gate in the fortress's outer wall. Following the cliff-edge, they climbed into deep woodland.

"I know the truth," the old man told Tom as they made their way through the trees. "I was there – a bold fellow in the prime of life. I saw it all." The shaman shook his head. "The final battle was dreadful carnage," he muttered. "So much death and destruction…"

"And at the end?" Tom asked.

The old man pushed through hanging branches. "The legends say that after his victory, the

Avantian conqueror and all his army vanished." He shook his head. "There *was* no army by the end. Every invading soldier lay dead on the ground, and the blood ran in rivers down the hillside."

"Everyone was dead?" asked Tom in surprise.

"All but Uthrain and Prince Angelo, and just a few of us," said the shaman. "High on the hill, the two warriors fought in single combat, hewing at one another from sunrise until burning noon."

Tom looked around, trying to imagine such a titanic battle. He could almost hear the ring of steel on steel, and the grunting and panting of the two mighty warriors.

"At last, Angelo got in a lucky blow and Uthrain fell," said the shaman. "Angelo was bloody from head to foot, but he was formidable still, and none dared go near him." The shaman looked at Tom. "Most fled – but I remained to see what the conqueror would do."

They came to a copse of gnarled trees, high on the hill. There was an area of clear earth in the copse, and at its centre stood a dome of grey rocks over which the tendrils of wiry plants had grown.

"What is this?" Tom asked.

"This is Prince Angelo's tomb," said the old man.

Tom stared at him. "It can't be!"

"It is," said the old man. "Uthrain was defeated, but Angelo's wounds were so great, his own death came swiftly afterwards." He grimaced. "I was weary of warfare. I thought that if their prince never returned, the Avantians would think twice before invading the Wildlands again. So I buried Angelo and spread the story among my people that he and his army had vanished by magic." He gave Tom a sly smile. "I told them the invaders would return if they ever took up arms again. My cunning plan kept the peace in the Wildlands for many years."

"What of the human sacrifices to Krotax?" Tom asked angrily.

The shaman shrugged. "Every peace must have its price."

"But you must be lying," Tom said. "Angelo is alive and sitting on the throne of Avantia."

The shaman pointed at the piled rocks. "Believe your own eyes."

Tom strode across the clearing and began to heave the rocks away, quickly revealing a stone sarcophagus.

"The truth is inside," said the shaman.

Tom paused, staring down at the sarcophagus. *Is it right to disturb the dead?* But he had to know! He slid his sword under the lid and prised the slab off the stone coffin.

Inside was a skeleton, clad in dented armour, with bony hands folded across its chest. It had clearly been eaten away by the years. The raw skull grinned up at him.

"That's Avantian armour," breathed Tom, leaning closer and staring at a ring encircling the forefinger of the right hand. The stench of decay filled his head. There was something horrible about

being so close to the age-gnawed body.

I know that ring – I've seen a picture of it in the Archives!

It was a lost heirloom of Avantia – the golden ring of the old King Theo, given to his son Angelo when he went to war in the north.

Tom's mind reeled. "If this is Angelo's body," he murmured, "then the man seated on Avantia's throne is an imposter."

He could hardly take this in. Everything that had happened since Angelo had ridden up to the Royal Palace was based on lies!

Tom turned to the south, gazing towards his homeland.

"I will bring you down, deceiver!" he shouted. "While there is blood in my veins, I vow this – I will not rest until you are defeated!"

THE END

CONGRATULATIONS, YOU HAVE COMPLETED THIS QUEST!

At the end of each chapter you were awarded a special gold coin.
The QUEST in this book was worth an amazing 8 coins.

Look at the Beast Quest totem picture inside the back cover of this book to see how far you've come in your journey to become

MASTER OF THE BEASTS.

The more books you read, the more coins you will collect!

Do you want your own Beast Quest Totem?
1. Cut out and collect the coin below
2. Go to the Beast Quest website
3. Download and print out your totem
4. Add your coin to the totem
www.beastquest.co.uk/totem

550+ COINS
MASTER OF THE BEASTS

410 COINS
HERO

350 COINS
WARRIOR

230 COINS
KNIGHT

180 COINS
SQUIRE

44 COINS
PAGE

8 COINS
APPRENTICE

550+
515
480
445
410
395
380
365
350
328
290
260
230
217
206
191
180
146
112
78
44
30
19
8

READ ALL THE BOOKS IN SERIES 23:
THE SHATTERED KINGDOM!

BeastQuest
NEW BLOOD
ADAM BLADE

Meet three new heroes with the power to tame the Beasts!

Amy, Charlie and Sam – three children from our world – are about to discover the powerful legacy that binds them together.

They are descendants of the *Guardians of Avantia*, an elite group of heroes trained by Tom himself.

Now the time has come for a new generation to unlock the power of the Beasts and fulfil their destiny.

Read on for a sneak peek at how the Guardians first left Avantia by magic…

Karita of Banquise gazed in awe at Tom, Avantia's mighty, bearded Master of the Beasts.

Under his leadership, she and her companions would today face their greatest challenge.

Tom pointed towards the brooding Gorgonian castle. "We must recover the chest of Beast Eggs Malvel stole," he reminded them. His fierce blue eyes moved from Karita to the others. Dell of Stonewin, whose bloodline connected him to Beasts of Fire; Fern of Errinel, linked to Storm Beasts; Gustus of Colton, bonded with Water Beasts.

"Malvel will be expecting an attack," Tom said. "His power is lessened, but he is still formidable." His eyes locked on Karita. "Stealth will be our greatest ally."

Karita felt as though her whole life had been a preparation for this moment. Countless hours spent studying the ancient tomes, day after day of gruelling combat training, months learning how to influence the will of Stealth Beasts and control the powers that filled the Arcane Band at her wrist.

But was she ready?

She gazed into Tom's face, and her doubts faded.

Yes!

A low rumble came from the

castle. Flashes of green lightning shot from the clouds as a swarm of screeching creatures erupted from the battlements.

Karita shuddered as Malvel's hideous minions streaked through the sky. They were man-sized, with white hides, limbs tipped with hooked claws and gaping jaws lined with sharp teeth. Their leathery wings cracked like whips.

"Karrakhs!" muttered Tom. "Karita – go!"

She nodded and slipped away behind jagged rocks. She turned to see the swarm of foul creatures engulf her companions. Tom's sword flashed. Howls rang out from the Karrakhs. The Guardians were using their Arcane Bands to form weapons that spun and slashed!

Karita raced for the castle, keeping low behind the ridge of rocks. Reaching the walls, she climbed up a gnarled vine and found a narrow window to crawl through. She looked back again. Tom and the Guardians had battled their way through the castle gates.

Well fought!

She dropped into a room and crept to the door. Torches burned in the corridor, casting shadows. The castle was silent, but Karita felt a growing dread as she slipped along the walls.

She knew where the chest of Beast eggs was hidden. But would Malvel allow her to get to them?

She came to a circular room, and saw the chest standing by the wall. Her heart hammering, Karita opened the lid and gazed down at the eggs. They were different sizes, shapes and colours. One slipped from the pile and she caught it in her gloved hand. It was pale blue, about the size of a goose egg. Acting on instinct, she slipped it inside her breastplate.

Crash!

She spun around. Malvel stood against the room's closed door.

"Did you really think you could enter my domain unseen?" he snarled, a green glow igniting in his palm. His voice was weaker than she'd imagined. "I *wanted* you to come here. After all, only a Guardian can hatch a Beast Egg."

Karita swallowed hard, seeking a way to escape.

"You and your friends will hatch these Beasts and I will drink in their power," growled the wizard. "I will become mighty again and Avantia will bow before me!"

"I'm not afraid of you!" Karita shouted.

A ball of green fire exploded from Malvel's hand. Karita dived aside, seared by the heat.

She leaped up, thrusting her right arm towards the wizard. The Arcane Band began to form a weapon, but another blast of fire sent her sliding across the floor.

Malvel loomed over her, both hands

burning green. Before he could strike, the door burst open and Tom and the Guardians rushed into the room.

"No!" roared Malvel. "Where are my Karrakhs?"

"Defeated!" shouted Tom, whirling his sword to deflect Malvel's green flames. "Guardians! Take the eggs!"

Fern dived for the chest, but a blast from the wizard knocked her over.

"The eggs are mine!" howled Malvel. He traced a large circle of fire in the air. There was a blast of hot wind as the flaming hoop crackled and spat.

Malvel snatched up the chest and turned to the heart of the fiery circle.

"He's opened a portal!" shouted

Tom. "Stop him!"

Gustus ran at the wizard and wrested the chest from his grip. Roaring in anger, Malvel launched a fireball, but Fern managed to shove Gustus out of its path. But the force of her push knocked Gustus into the portal. With a stifled cry, he and the chest of eggs were gone.

"No!" Fern shouted, diving in after him. With a shout, Dell ran after her.

"Wait!" shouted Tom.

"It's our duty to protect the eggs!" Dell called back as he disappeared into the swirling portal.

Malvel sprang forward, but Tom bounded in front of him, holding him back with his spinning blade as the wizard hurled magical fireballs.

Karita saw the walls of the portal writhing and distorting. Malvel's fireballs were making it unstable. At any moment it might vanish!

Tom was knocked back by a torrent of green fire as the wizard turned and leaped into the portal. Karita flung herself after him.

"No! Karita!" The last thing she heard was Tom's voice. "The portal is in flux! You could be sent anywhere!"

And then there was nothing but a rushing wind and howling darkness, as she plunged into the unknown.

Look out for
Beast Quest: New Blood
to find out what happens next!